BRONCO DOGS

by Caron Lee Cohen

pictures by Roni Shepherd

DUTTON CHILDREN'S BOOKS NEW YORK

Library of Congress Cataloging-in-Publication Data
Cohen, Caron Lee.
Bronco dogs / Caron Lee Cohen; pictures by Roni Shepherd.
—1st ed.
p. cm.
Summary: Bank robbers Sixgun Gus and Cannonball Clyde
get into the worst trouble ever and become ghosts
but remain best friends.
ISBN 0-525-44721-0
[1. Robbers and outlaws—Fiction. 2. Dogs—Fiction.
3. Ghosts—Fiction. 4. West (U.S.)—Fiction.]
I. Shepherd, Roni, ill. II. Title.
PZ7.C65974Br 1991
[E]—dc20 90-47952 CIP AC

Published in the United States by Dutton Children's Books,
a division of Penguin Books USA Inc.
Designer: Susan Phillips
Printed in Hong Kong
First Edition 10 9 8 7 6 5 4 3 2 1

For Stan and Judy Levine,
and also for Golda David and
Melody Siroty, the dream nurturers

C.L.C.

To Morgan, my son,
and to Baron and Red, my own
favorite Bronco Dogs

R.S.

Sixgun Gus and Cannonball Clyde were wilder than the wildest broncos, and they had dogs' manners, so the folks around Sacramento called them the Bronco Dogs. Those Bronco Dogs held up banks and stagecoaches and even the Pony Express.

It wasn't easy being bad guys. They were always riding and running and running and riding and shooting their guns all the way from Sacramento to Death Valley, where they'd hide out.

Sixgun Gus was hard as a devil's horn. He liked to sleep outside under the moonlight in the craters of volcanoes, in the hills, in the canyons, or on the salt flats somewhere near Badwater in the sink of the Amargosa River.

Now, Cannonball Clyde was a little more softheaded. He had a hankering for a real cozyish bed and a hot-water bath, but no innkeeper anywhere in California would let those dogs in. So once a month the Bronco Dogs went clear to Texas so Cannonball could bed down and take a bath.

Not so Sixgun. He liked his doggie odor.

It was a lonely life, but at least those Bronco Dogs had each other. Many a day Cannonball would say to Sixgun, "Uh, doggone! And lasso my tail! We ain't nothin' without each other!"

"Good golly! Doggies be danged!" Sixgun would add, "We're best friends—*dead or alive!*"

They were best friends all right, stuck together like glue, until they got into the worst dog-dang trouble. It all started the afternoon they held up the First Cowgirl Bank in Sacramento, looking to make their biggest haul ever—twenty-one pounds of gold each!

With her hands up, one bank teller stopped Sixgun. "Everyone knows," she said in a whisper, "in the end, a bad dog will never rest!"

"Oh, dog water," said Sixgun.

Then he and Cannonball jumped on their horses and hot-hoofed it right out of there, barely keeping in front of a herd of cowgirls.

For days and nights and nights and days the Bronco Dogs were riding and running and running and riding and shooting their guns across the craters of volcanoes, across the hills, the canyons, and the salt flats toward somewhere near Badwater in the sink of the Amargosa River.

Every time the dogs looked back, they saw the cowgirls riding after them.

"Good gravy!" said Cannonball. "We need something to, uh, scare them off."

"There's one thing could scare off the whole bunch of 'em!" said Sixgun. "*A ghost!*"

"Uh, trouble is, ya can never find one when ya need one," said Cannonball, "and those cowgirls just keep comin'!"

"That's why we gotta just keep goin'. Let's git!"

So that's what they did. But at the top of Coma-ti-yi-yippi-yippi-yea Peak, Cannonball Clyde fell right off. He fell all 14,492 feet down the side of that cliff.

"*Oh, no! Cannonball Cly-y-y-y-y-de!*" Sixgun screamed, and quick as lightning he swung his lasso. Then he got scared out of his waistcoat, for sure as shootin' he had lassoed . . .

A GHOST!

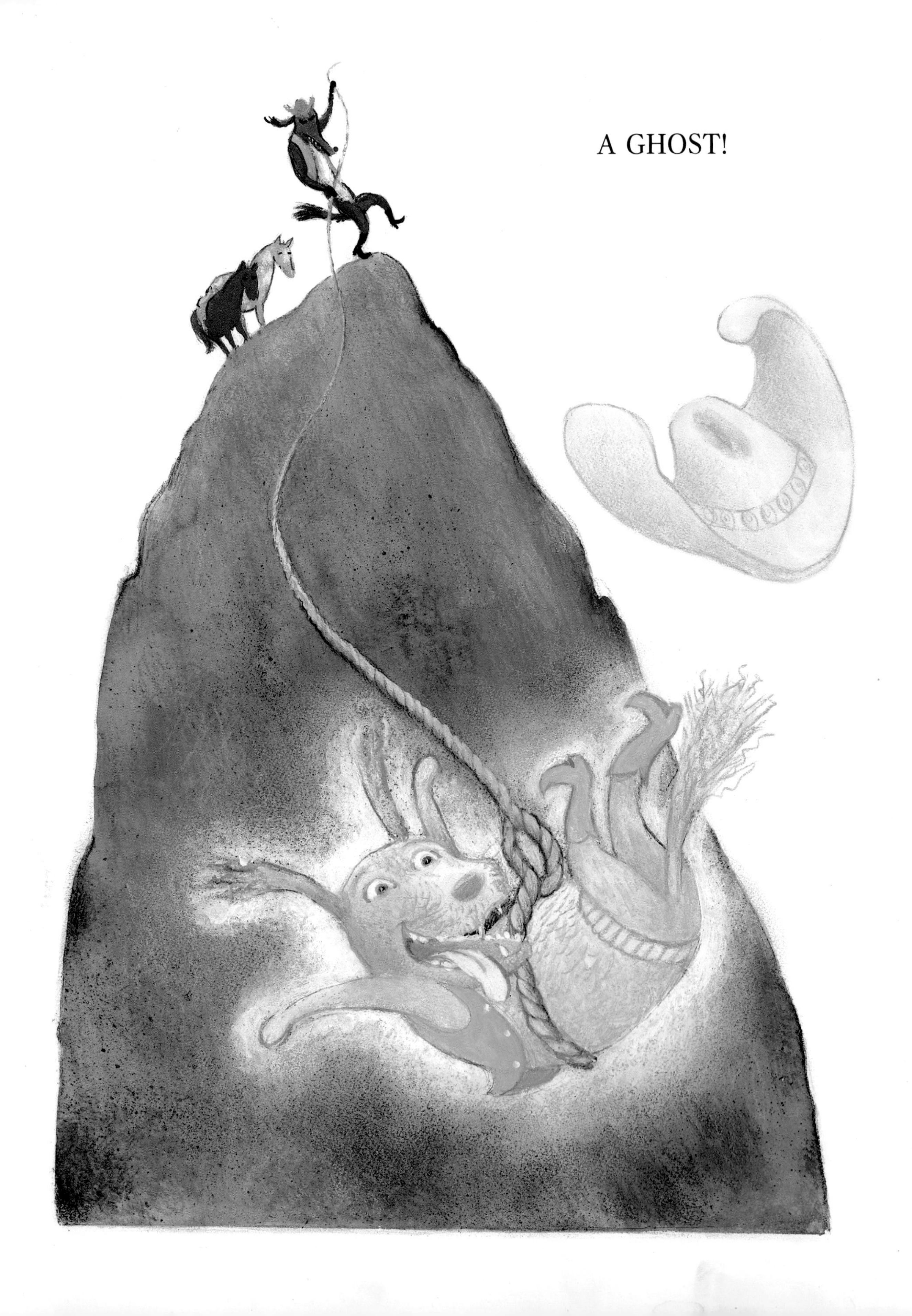

When he finally calmed down, he saw that the ghost was Cannonball. Sixgun cried and cried for his partner.

"There, there. Uh, dry those tears," said Cannonball. "We're still best friends—*dead or alive!* And now I'm just what we, uh, needed—*a ghost.* I can protect our gold."

So Sixgun cheered up, kissed that ghost square on the nose, and pronto, buried the gold.

"I'll stay right here, pardner," said Cannonball the ghost, "so you know where to find me. You hide till those cowgirls are gone."

Sixgun said, "Giddyup horsey," and rode off.

Cannonball was true to his word. When those cowgirls got there, he shouted, "Uh . . . *Boo!*"

That scared the skirts off them! Those cowgirls
lit out quicker than a herd of stampeding bulls!

Pretty soon word got around Sacramento that there was a ghost protecting a stash of gold in Death Valley. It was just old Cannonball, keeping his word and waiting for Sixgun to come back.

Time went by. The news of the hidden gold spread as far north as Fort Walla Walla, and back east to Cuyahoga, Ohio. Cowboys, cowgirls, cowpokes, and a couple of cows came to get it. They all turned out to be cowards—scared out of their skins by Cannonball.

As more time passed, Cannonball Clyde got sadder and sadder. He was bored silly scaring folks. He wanted a bath and a cozyish bed. But he could never sleep nohow. Night after night the words of that bank teller came back to him. *A bad dog will never rest!*

But dad-blasted, worse than anything else he missed his partner real bad and couldn't help remembering all the good times they had together.

Then one afternoon Cannonball thought he saw a ghost. And good golly, it was Sixgun Gus! "Well, I'll be! Yippy! Yippy! Uh, Yippy! It's Sixgun, my pardner!" They hugged each other tight.

"Why, uh, you're no dog. You're a ghost! Ain't ya," said Cannonball.

"That's right," said Sixgun. "And I'm glad to be one, 'cause now I'm with you, Cannonball. We're best friends—*dead or alive!*"

"Well, uh, jeepers, what happened?" asked Cannonball.

"My horsey just didn't giddyup fast enough, so those cowgirls caught me and stuck me in jail. I spent night after night in a cell as dark as a wolf's mouth. Finally they said they couldn't stand my doggie odor, so I had to take a bath. But I slipped on the soap and drowned in that there tub! So here I am—a doggone ghost, same as you. I sure am lookin' forward to sleepin' outside under the moonlight like in the old days."

Cannonball started to cry. "Oh, Sixgun, you old ghost. You're a bad dog, and so am I. Neither of us will ever sleep again. Uh, I ain't slept since that dog-dang day at the Cowgirl Bank. *And it's terrible.*"

"That bad, huh?" said Sixgun. "You figure we could just give all the loot back and go the straight and narrow? And then get us a good night's sleep?"

Cannonball shook his head. "Ain't nobody gonna get close enough to a couple of ghosts for us to give it to 'em."

Sixgun thought and thought. And then he came up with a plan.

The Bronco Dogs dug up all the gold and started hauling it over the salt flats, and the hills, and the canyons, and the craters of volcanoes.

They were riding and running and running and riding and hauling that loot until they came to Sacramento, where all the living folks hollered and ran—just like Cannonball said they would.

They walked right up and into the First Cowgirl Bank and left the gold on the president's desk with a note.

In no time flat the cowgirls came and read the note and said they'd give the gold back to the folks who'd been robbed.

As the Bronco Dogs took off out of town, Cannonball said, "Uh, sure feels good bein' good guys for a change!"

"Sure does, don't it!" said Sixgun.

Since then, Sixgun Gus has been sleeping outside under the moonlight, just the way he likes. And right next to him, Cannonball Clyde has a real heavenish bed and a bathtub too, just the way *he* likes. Those Bronco Dogs are resting in peace and happiness together. And they will be forever.